My Name is

...........................

I don't care
if you like
my name or not.
*That's* my name.
It's the only
name I've got.

# MY Book about ME

## By ME MYSELF

I wrote it!
I drew it!
with a little help from my friends

### Dr. Seuss and Roy McKie

COLLINS

I CAN READ IT ALL BY MYSELF

**Beginner Books**

Trademark of Random House, Inc., William Collins Sons & Co. Ltd., Authorised User

4 5 6 7 8 9 10

ISBN 0 00 171401 5 (paperback)

ISBN 0 00 171404 X (hardback)

Copyright © 1969 by Dr Seuss
A Beginner Book published by arrangement with
Random House Inc., New York, New York
First published in Great Britain 1973

Printed & bound in Hong Kong

# MY BOOK
## about ME

# First of all

there is one thing
you should know.

Am I a boy?
Or am I a girl?

Well,
I'll tell you.

## I am a

........................

I weigh _____ kilograms.

How tall am I?

I am __ centimetres

tall.

# My Teeth

I counted them.

I have _____ up top.

I have ___ downstairs.

# My Hair looks like this:

I drew it in.

 Straight hair

 Curly hair

 Long hair

 Short hair

Pony tail

Brown hair

Red hair

White hair

Grey hair

 Blonde hair

Black hair

Purple hair

Green hair

Orange hair

 No hair

4

# My Hand is this big.

(I drew around it with a pencil.)

# Do you want to know
# how big **My Foot** is?

Well, this is how big.

(I drew around it with a pencil.)

Long nose

Short nose

Up nose

Down nose

Broken nose

# My Nose

THIS is how my nose goes.

I drew it.

8

# My Eyes

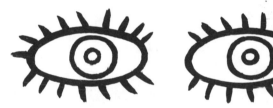

**THIS** is the colour of my eyes.

 Blue eyes

 Brown eyes

 Green eyes

 Black eyes

 Pink eyes

 Hazel eyes

 Grey eyes

 Yellow eyes

9

# Eyeglasses

I wear glasses. ☐

Tick one.

I don't wear glasses. ☐

10

# FRECKLES

I don't wear freckles. ☐

Tick one.

I do wear freckles. ☐

I think I have about_____ freckles.

# Where in the world do I live?

## I live in one of these countries.

| | | | |
|---|---|---|---|
| Afghanistan | Botswana | Congo (Brazzaville) | Ethiopia |
| Albania | Brazil | Costa Rica | Finland |
| Algeria | Bulgaria | Cuba | France |
| Andorra | Burma | Cyprus | |
| Angola | Burundi | Czechoslovakia | |
| Argentina | | | Gabon |
| Australia | | | Gambia |
| Austria | Cambodia | Dahomey | Germany (East) |
| | Cameroon | Denmark | Germany (West) |
| Bahrain | Canada | Dominican Republic | Ghana |
| Bangladesh | Central African Republic | | Great Britain |
| Barbados | Chad | | Greece |
| Belgium | Chile | Ecuador | Guatemala |
| Bhutan | China | Egypt | Guinea |
| Bolivia | Colombia | El Salvador | Guyana |

| | | | |
|---|---|---|---|
| Haiti | Libya | Pakistan | Switzerland |
| Honduras | Liechtenstein | Panama | Syria |
| Hungary | Luxembourg | Paraguay | |
| | | Peru | Taiwan |
| Iceland | | Philippines | Tanzania |
| India | Malagasy Republic | Poland | Thailand |
| Indonesia | Malawi | Portugal | Togo |
| Iran | Malaysia | | Trinidad and Tobago |
| Iraq | Maldive Islands | Qatar | Trucial States |
| Ireland | Mali | | Tunisia |
| Israel | Malta | Rhodesia | Turkey |
| Italy | Mauritania | Romania | |
| Ivory Coast | Mauritius | Russia | |
| | Mexico | Rwanda | Uganda |
| | Monaco | | United States |
| Jamaica | Mongolia | San Marino | Upper Volta |
| Japan | Morocco | Saudi Arabia | Uruguay |
| Jordan | Mozambique | Senegal | |
| | Muscat and Oman | Sierra Leone | Vatican City |
| Kenya | | Sikkim | Venezuela |
| Korea (North) | | Singapore | Vietnam |
| Korea (South) | Nepal | Somalia | |
| Kuwait | Netherlands | South Africa | Western Samoa |
| | New Zealand | Spain | |
| Laos | Nicaragua | Sri Lanka | Yemen |
| Lebanon | Niger | Sudan | Yugoslavia |
| Lesotho | Nigeria | Swaziland | |
| Liberia | Norway | Sweden | Zambia |

I live in

13

If you want to send me a letter
here's my name and address.

If you want to phone me,
call this number:

_____

# My House

Block of flats          House in the city

House in a town

House in the country

House in the mountains

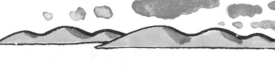

House in the desert

House in the suburbs

Farm house

House near the water

Igloo

## The house I live in is:

_____

# My House

has ———— windows.

My house has ———— beds.

My house has ———— pictures on the walls.

## My house

has _____ steps.

There are _____ forks in my house

## My house has

_____ keyholes.

In my house, there are _____ lights.

We have _____ clocks.

In my house, there are ———— mirrors.

We have ———— cold water taps and ———— hot.

# About ME and EATING

I eat like a horse. ☐

I eat
like a bird. ☐

I eat like a _____ ☐

My favourite food is

_____

and _____

and _____

And please
*don't* give me any

_____

I can't stand it.

# My Birthday

is

Month _____

Day _____

Next year
I will have ____ candles.

I drew in
the right number
of candles.

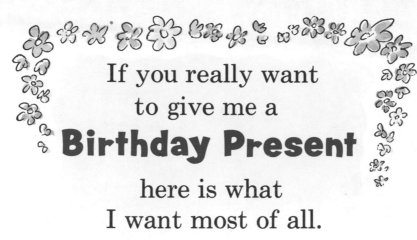

If you really want
to give me a
# Birthday Present
here is what
I want most of all.

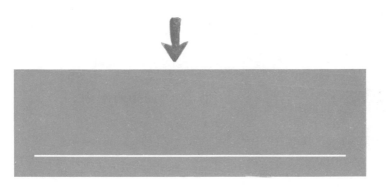

(But if it costs
too much,
forget it.)

# I Go to School

I go on foot. ☐

I go on my bike. ☐

I go by helicopter. ☐

I go by bus. ☐

I go by car. ☐

I go by underground. ☐

I go by _____ ☐

My favourite teacher's name is

_____

Reading   Maths

Spelling   Art

Writing

Music

I study many things.

I like _____ best.

I like _____ worst.

I am a very good student. ☐

I am a so-so student. ☐

I am awful. ☐

# Here are some more interesting things about ME

I have read about _____ books.

My favourite book is _____

I am right handed. ☐

☐ I am left handed.

☐ I am both handed. ☐

I can stand on my hands

for _____ seconds.

My feet are ticklish

YES ☐

NO ☐

Dog Cat

Bird

Monkey

Alligator

Guinea Pig

# My Favourite Pet

Pig

Fish

Hamster

Pony

Horse

Gerbil

Bear

Turtle

Donkey

Snake

Goat

Skunk

Mouse

Rat

Squirrel

Toad

Octopus

## is _____

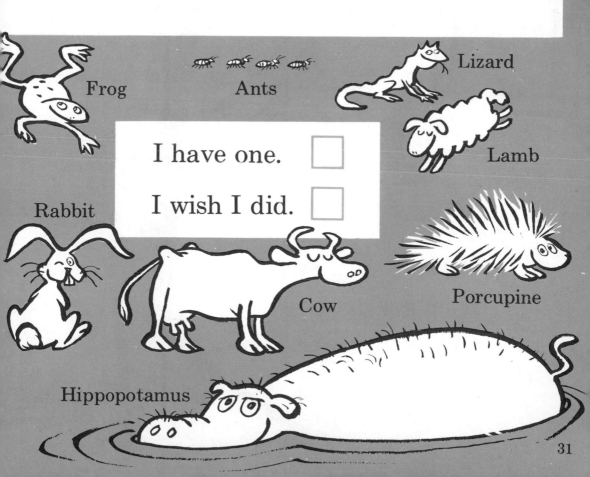

Frog

Ants

Lizard

Lamb

I have one. ☐

I wish I did. ☐

Rabbit

Cow

Porcupine

Hippopotamus

31

# Some Secret Things I Know

It is _____ steps
from my door
to the first tree.

It is _____ steps
from my tree
to the first letterbox.

It is _____ steps
from my letterbox.
to the first store.

I bet YOU never knew *that* before!

# My Clothes

I own exactly _____ buttons.

And I counted my zips.

I have _____ zips.

My
Favourite Colour
is

_____

# My Very Special Autograph Collection

Most kids can't get them all.

_____

An uncle's autograph

_____

An aunt's autograph

_____

A cousin's autograph

_____

Our postman's autograph

_____    _____

A grandmother's                    A grandfather's

A fireman's autograph

A market man's autograph

A policeman's autograph

A delivery man's autograph

Autograph of a man with a beard.

Autograph of a man more than 2 metres tall.

# My Best Friend

## is

a boy ☐

a dog ☐

☐ a cat

☐ a girl

My best friend's name is:

_____

Here is how to spell it backwards:

_____

# Sometimes

## I Get Mad at Some People

YES   NO

Tick one.

I kicked someone.

YES   NO

I pushed someone.

YES    NO

I hit someone.

YES    NO

I yanked hair.

YES    NO

I'm sorry I did it.

YES

NO

# My Longests

My longest walk was _____ kilometres.

My longest bike ride was _____ kilometres.

My longest car trip was
_____ kilometres.

My longest plane trip.
_____ kilometres.

My longest fish was

_____ centimetres.

My longest swim was

_____ metres.

My longest hair.

is __ centimetres.

I CAN DRAW
funny pictures
like this

# I drew this bird

His name is _____

# My Hobbies

## I collect

  stamps

 sea shells

 birds' eggs

 nothing

46

coins ☐

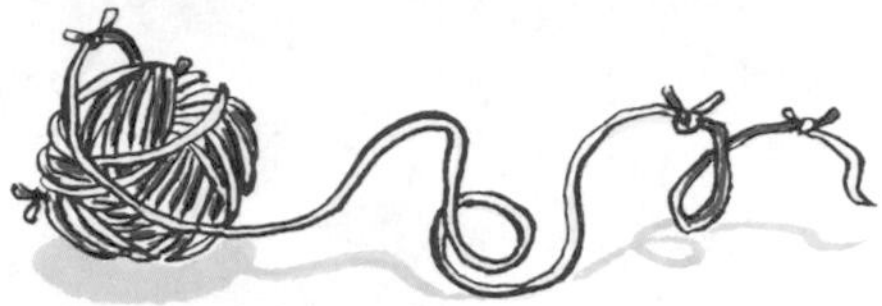

string ☐

butterflies ☐

walrus whiskers ☐

# What else?

I collect _____

_____

47

# My Favourite Sport is

_____

I am very good. ☐

I am sort of good. ☐

I am not so good. ☐

# My Favourite Song is

I sing in my bath.

 YES  NO

Tick one.

I am a great whistler.

 YES  NO

I hum better than I whistle.

 YES  NO

Guitar

Xylophone

Trumpet

Cello

Violin

Trombone

Drums

Piano

My Favourite
Musical Instrument
is

# I am

Very neat ☐

Not so neat ☐

Pretty sloppy ☐

I talk in my sleep. ☐

I never talk in my sleep. ☐

I like to get up
at _____ o'clock.

# I can make NOISES

like a rooster ☐

like a dog ☐

like a cat ☐

like a goat ☐

like a sheep ☐

like a goose ☐

like a train ☐

like a _____

like a _____

like a _____

My family loves
my noises.

YES    NO

| Farmer | Plumber | Electrician | Cook |
|--------|---------|-------------|------|
| Doctor | Carpenter | Fireman | Pilot |
| Nurse | Secretary | Policeman | Writer |

# When I Grow Up, I Want to

| Lion Tamer | Cowboy | Football Player |
|------------|--------|-----------------|
| Lorry Driver | Indian | Hairdresser |
| Astronaut | Frogman | Dress designer |
| Mechanic | Painter | Mathematician |
| Violinist | Barman | Stockbroker |
| Taxi Driver | Baseball Player | Movie Star |
| Minister | T.V. Star | Photographer |
| Priest | | Telephone Operator |
| Nun | | |
| Steeplejack | | Horticulturist |
| Librarian | | Paleontologist |
| Musician | | Coal Miner |
| Burglar | | Gold Miner |
| | | Rabbi |

| Artist | Actor | Tailor | Teacher |
| Dentist | Banker | Soldier | Nothing |
| Postman | Lawyer | Sailor | Dancer |

# Be _____

| Judge | Gardener | Millionaire |
| Jockey | Senator | Singer |
| Jeweller | General | Cartoonist |
| President | Butcher | Locksmith |
| Milkman | Sculptor | Blacksmith |
| Accountant | Pianist | Salesman |
| Air Hostess | Acrobat | Shopkeeper |
| Mother | Watchmaker | Fisherman |
| Magician | Dog Trainer | Statistician |
| Mayor | Explorer | Veterinarian |
| Sea Captain | Manufacturer | Zymologist |
| Window Cleaner | | Yak Trainer |
| Bus Driver | | |
| Camel Driver | | |

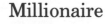

# I Like to Write Stories

Here is one I wrote.

Good story, isn't it?

# Well, sir! That's MY Book About ME.

I finished writing it

_____ Month

_____ Day

_____ Year

# HI!

I'm back again.

Here are three things about Me
I forgot to tell you.

I own ———— shoelaces.

and

I own ————— buttonholes.

and

I wish
I were a giraffe. ☐

I'm glad
I'm not a giraffe. ☐